TWISTED TALES

AMAZING ADVENTURES

Edited By Wendy Laws

First published in Great Britain in 2022 by:

 Young**Writers**®
Est. 1991

Young Writers
Remus House
Coltsfoot Drive
Peterborough
PE2 9BF
Telephone: 01733 890066
Website: www.youngwriters.co.uk

Printed and bound in the UK by BookPrintingUK
Website: www.bookprintinguk.com
YB0501P

FOREWORD

Welcome, Reader!

Come into our lair, there's really nothing to fear. You may have heard bad things about the villains within these pages, but there's more to their stories than you might think...

For our latest competition, Twisted Tales, we challenged secondary school students to write a story in just 100 words that shows us another side to the traditional storybook villain. We asked them to look beyond the evil escapades and tell a story that shows a bad guy or girl in a new light. They were given optional story starters for a spark of inspiration, and could focus on their motivation, back story, or even what they get up to in their downtime!

And that's exactly what the authors in this anthology have done, giving us some unique new insights into those we usually consider the villain of the piece. The result is a thrilling and absorbing collection of stories written in a variety of styles, and it's a testament to the creativity of these young authors.

Here at Young Writers it's our aim to inspire the next generation and instill in them a love of creative writing, and what better way than to see their work in print? The imagination and skill within these pages are proof that we might just be achieving that aim! Congratulations to each of these fantastic authors.

CONTENTS

Sophie Brady (11)	51
Amelie Gwynn (12)	52
Jacob Shipp (11)	53
Riley Wakefield (11)	54
Jed Rundle (12)	55
Eli Phelan (11)	56
Finley Griffee (11)	57
Magda Wickiewicz (11)	58
Finlay Jouxson (14)	59
Cole Rogerson (12)	60

D'Overbroecks College, Oxford

Mariia Lysenko (15)	61
Sze Long (15)	62
Alisa Arkharova (13)	63
Jun Theppadungporn (14)	64
Derrick Lam (14)	65
Howard Pang (14)	66
Harry Wang (13)	67

Danesgate Community PRU, Danesgate

Hayden Gell (14)	68

Dixon Fazakerley Academy, Aintree

Stefan Pinzaru (14)	69
Wealth Okojie-Aiyagbonrhuele (14)	70
Louie Dunbabin (14)	71
Marty McCarthy (14)	72

Eastbourne College, Eastbourne

Tsz Yin, Isaac Lee (13)	73
Lucy O'Hara	74
Serena Ting (14)	75
Poppy Campion (13)	76
Felix Boyes	77
Orlando Soucek (13)	78
Olivia Wilson (14)	79
Emilia Dixon (13)	80

Myles Luther (13)	81
Theo Hazlewood (14)	82
Dom Muschialli (13)	83
Nicholas Beech	84
Nancy Revill	85
Dan Clark	86
Libby Thorley (13)	87
Lily Michaelides (14)	88
Bertie Kane (14)	89
Alex Pilsbury (14)	90
William Bligh	91
Alfie Lulham (14)	92
Freddie Russell	93

Felpham Community College, Felpham

Grace Hill (14)	94
Annalise Towse (14)	95
Reece Bevan (12)	96
Katy Pilling (13)	97
Max Broad (13)	98
Jacob Miles (13)	99
Dylan Woods (13)	100
Scarlett Whittle (13)	101

George Abbot School, Burpham

Verity Lowndes (13)	102
Jasmine Lee (12)	103
Hayley Genge (11)	104
Manaswini Venugopal (12)	105
Amber Grundy (11)	106
Daniel Chen (11)	107

Haberdashers' Aske's Boys' School, Elstree

Joshi Lappin (13)	108
David Gluhovsky (12)	109
Oliver Broadwith (13)	110
Ishaan Shah (12)	111
Arav Bahel (13)	112
Vivaan Chhabra (12)	113

THE
STORIES

ABOVE THEIR REALITY

Every day is the same. Same stochastic bloodshed. Everyone was paranoid to death, like literally. Why wasn't I? Puzzled, I burn the remains. People are just overreacting. Try being me. Some days, I was an ordinary being: one side of me a civilian, the other a hopeless killer. Life was too easy. I faced not a single threat. I wasn't a mere mortal; thus the deceased only nourished my life span. "I'm an immortal being," I mumbled, resting in a warm puddle of my own sacred blood. Life became boring. Oh, what boredom does to oneself, the puddle turning cold.

Nia Sarova (13)
ACS International School, Cobham

BETRAYAL

The madness, the anger, the taste of betrayal scorching down the back of my throat... I know what you think of me. Psychopath. Evil. Heartless. But you're wrong. He, with the golden hair and dazzling smiles; the hero. Do you know him? Trust him, really? Or are you blinded by his false heroic acts? Well, let me answer that for you; yes.

The scarlet stains my fingers as I look at the lifeless heap in front of me. Sunshine hair and toned arms. Fake. Counterfeit. Lies. I kneel down into the crimson pool. "Revenge, dear brother."

Psychopath? Evil? Heartless? Maybe.

Tamsyn Sayles
Amery Hill School, Amery Hill

A BLOOD FEUD

Here I lay; rejected. Alone. Stripped of everything - all hope. How was I to live? Pitiful. He'd won. He'd taken it all. None left - not for me. A blood feud - to end with only one victor. He will forsake me. My name will be disgraced. Vanquished by my brother, how foolish. He will stamp me in the mud at his feet, my people will betray me and hail him. Traitors! All of them.

Revenge was no option, not when I was so crippled. Done for. I must accept. But I'll never forget. Not what he'd done. It couldn't be forgiven.

Sophie Moore (13)
Amery Hill School, Amery Hill

MEDUSA

"Come out, Gorgon!" he called, smugly. "Come out so I may slay you where you stand."
Inhale. Exhale. How did he find her? Her mind was racing. No one had dared enter Libya since the curse. She had been placing offerings when it happened. A huge hand had clamped her mouth and her tunic was jerked and pulled. It wasn't that that haunted her. The feeling of her hair receding as it was replaced with the writhing creatures that now sit atop her head haunted her. "Where are you hiding, creature?"
Inhale. Exhale. She stepped into the open.

Alisha Child (14)
Beacon Academy, Crowborough

4

THE QUARRY

The night is clear and I wait for my quarry to appear. Scotland has been thrown into chaos; the late king's body was still warm when the crown was stolen from his head. Soon afterwards, I lost my job and I was forced to kill to make enough to put food on the table. What will my children think when they learn how many lives their father has taken? A movement attracts my attention. Banquo. I spring upon him and watch as the life drains out of him. I shall make haste to Dunsinane to report this to the King.

Amelia Beecroft
Beacon Academy, Crowborough

DEATH

There are over a billion people in this world, and death is, or will be, a part of everyone's life. I completely understand that I'm not everyone's cup of tea, however, death is a part of life.

Sometimes, when somebody dies, someone else gets the blame. Honestly, I get no credit!

One time I saw someone wearing socks with sandals so they just had to go.

I get confused sometimes because when people say the words "kill me" I think, *are you joking?* Because I can grant your wish. What I'm trying to say is, I'm not the bad guy.

Beatrice Musselwhite Knell (14)
Box Hill School, Mickleham

DESTROYER OF HUMANS

The essence of joy was sucked from the land as 'Golgorath the Devourer of Life' trudged down from his cave on high and turned the villages to smoking rubble. Golgorath was a giant, hideous green ogre who destroyed anything in his path. He had decimated the land of Minhirich for a millennium making the place a barren wasteland. His kind was hunted by the people he now oppresses. He slaughters every human he can find in revenge for what they did. He would starve and torture people to make them suffer just for his amusement. Nothing survived his devastating rampage.

Michael Carroll (15)
Box Hill School, Mickleham

MIRROR, MIRROR

I never really belonged. "Ugly, hideous and creepy," everyone called me that. Hit, bullied and tormented by the rich, especially by the future King! My life felt like a downhill spiral, never ever going right. I would go home crying, wishing to be beautiful and cursing the King's kingdom and that one day I would snatch it. When I was older, I changed my looks, plotted and tried to find spells to take my revenge although none worked. When the King's child, Snow White, turned one I came across a mirror quietly telling me how I could fulfil my wish...

Evie Daniel (14)
Box Hill School, Mickleham

THE HALLOWEEN CLOWN

Bow ties, make-up and big feet weren't always a part of me. On the night of October 31st, it all went wrong. Painting my face in white, I noticed a slight reaction on my skin but I continued. Slamming the door behind, Halloween had begun! *Bang!* I had hit my head from tripping over my stupid clown shoes. Gingerly opening my eyes, a strong stench of sewage swept across my nose. "Where am I?" I asked myself. Suddenly, evil laughs echoed through the endless tunnels. Feeling anxious, I curled up into a ball, thinking it would help. Will I escape?

Luca Fulco (14)
Box Hill School, Mickleham

WHY?

Waking up in a filthy tent every single tedious day, looking forward to nothing and only having my imagination to comfort me... The government forgot about the small majority of poverty-stricken people; this was me. Every day I had to steal to survive, just to eat scraps. As I got older and more adventurous, I got ambitious and dived into a life of crime. It's like we were aliens. The media told the 'Normals' that we were dangerous. They chased us out and violently killed my brothers. Now it's my turn to plot revenge. They will not have mercy...

Philip Puckett (14)
Box Hill School, Mickleham

DRACO'S REVENGE

After Harry had snapped the Elder Wand, Draco came out of nowhere and screamed, "It's not fair, you always get to have the happy ending."

Harry replied, "It's because I didn't choose the wrong side."

"Enough! I'm going to kill you." Draco killed Harry with a spell and threw his body off the bridge. Draco went to the main complex and burnt Hogwarts down, killing everyone in sight from kids to teachers. He went to Hagrid, locked him in and killed him by burning his house. He left with no one alive.

Jack Underwood
Box Hill School, Mickleham

THE VAMPIRE

The hate hurts. I have feelings too; I am not a monster. Just because I don't look like you; I don't do the things you do; I don't eat the things you do. It doesn't make me evil. I may drink blood, but I need to, to survive. You people are the real villains: destroying the planet, mass killing, leaving most of the world barely surviving while others thrive. Heck, you even kill each other, how stupid is that. I'm taking a break, going on holiday; Somewhere sunny, I'm obviously kidding. Please leave me, I want to be left alone.

Oliver Hopkinson (14)

Box Hill School, Mickleham

COLD, COLD HEART

"Wait!" I begged. The screams faded. "Listen..." I prayed. The dagger moved away. "When I was little, I visited a house. In it, there was a wardrobe. Inside, a whole new world. I saw a boy, his eyes lured me in. Soon, I left the house, but the memories didn't. Every time I thought of him, my heart felt warm." Tears set me on fire as I spoke. "Years passed, and I returned. We fell in love, but soon, my prince was gone. The crown put me in a cage, losing him broke my heart into shards of ice, forever..."

Ekaterina Chasounikova (14)
Box Hill School, Mickleham

TAKEN FOR GRANTED

As the ashes and embers drifted down all around me, blackened timbers crumbling to dust, I looked back at why I did this; if maybe I made the wrong choice. They did not care for me, a simple lover of stones and clean things. Day after day, hours were spent constraining majestic stone sculptures, only for the Ninky Nonk to run them down without a thought. I would sit in my cave, questioning my existence. None of them cared. Not one. I had had enough. I said to myself, "No longer shall this forest be one of wood, but one of stone."

Rory Simm (15)
Box Hill School, Mickleham

AN UGLY MAN AND AN UGLY WORLD

I was born a malicious, malformed monster. My parents feared me when I was born. At only two years old I was left at an orphanage. Growing up there was a hellish, hurtful and harrowing experience. My so-called peers described me as a demon from hell, Satan's scary, sadistic creation. Eventually, I grew numb to the abuse. When I turned nineteen I got out of that place, hoping that maybe someone on this earth would have some sympathy for me. But no. Nobody is that nice I suppose. So now I wear this mask, taking revenge on this world.

Adam Khan (15)
Box Hill School, Mickleham

LORD FARQUAAD'S REVENGE

As I watched Shrek, Fiona and Donkey celebrate after they saw me run away with my grey horse, I knew I should have gone back for revenge then.

Four days later I managed to capture Donkey, I grilled him to tell me everything that Fiona and Shrek had been saying about me. Once Donkey repeated what they said, it fuelled me up even more! I gathered my largest and strongest men to storm their small, little wooden shack. I told the soldiers everything Donkey told me. So, on Thursday, late that night, I gave my men the signal to storm!

Joshua King (15)
Box Hill School, Mickleham

ORPHAN

I never really belonged. I didn't look like all the other girls. My short, jet-black hair stood out amongst their golden locks. I was much taller than them all. Everywhere I went I could feel their icy gazes staring up at me, whispering. They hated me because of how I looked. They hated me because I was an orphan. That's why I hated Cinderella. Her long hair reminded me of all the girls who made my life a misery growing up. How was she so perfect? I shut her away because I saw those girls in her. 'Evil' Stepmother.

Carys Barnes (14)
Box Hill School, Mickleham

THE CANDLELIGHT

My plan was working... the old man lit the candle. He shuffled around and held it high for a bit and then stopped. I was watching from afar. The whole room was dark, with one stray beam of sunlight on the other side of the room, far away from the orange-yellow candlelight.

Now he slowly moved forwards and I followed, trying not to make any noise on the creaky floorboards and trying to avoid standing in the light and blowing my cover. The man walked to the window and looked out of it. He screamed out and dropped dead.

Gabriel Howland-Brocklehurst (14)

Box Hill School, Mickleham

THE GREEK BEAST

Asterion is my name, when I was born everybody loved me. I was destined to have a normal life, at least that's what I thought... I was seven, all alone in a dark forest, I heard screams. I ran as quick as I could in the other direction, but stumbled across a bear. I remember feeling something being ripped off my face. I was blind, I couldn't see. I collapsed in shock. When I woke I could see again. I was woken by screams, my face feeling hairy. People running from me. I'm the Minotaur. Only one of me now.

Samir Maharaj (15)
Box Hill School, Mickleham

DEATH'S AFTERLIFE

I know you question what I (Death) do in my free time. Well, I'm going to tell you anyways, I'm the creator of hell and it really annoys me when those brainless humans say that Satan is the creator, I made Satan! He's my son and when he can't do his simple job I have to clean up after him and it's tiring. I kill bad people and some good, it's sad when a good man is taken away, but I don't control it, the universe does. I just want one day where I could sit down and rest.

Abhinav Sojan (15)
Box Hill School, Mickleham

SACRIFICES

Call me a dictator, monster, villain. But nobody values human life more than me. Nobody.

Sacrifices...

Yes, there's beauty to freedom but it's ugly too; like you and me. I watched my brother die - I will not watch it happen again.

Sacrifices...

Five years. My exile.

Sacrifices...

Five years. Time since I proposed a plan that eliminated choice, but embedded peace in our society - a utopia.

Sacrifices...

Five years. How long politicians have mulled over my plan to create a perfect society.

Sacrifices...

Five days. How long politicians have to wait. Then I'll be back and this time I'll stay.

Kiera Probert
Brighton College, Brighton

FALLEN KING

The glistening city stood before me. Once, the emperor denounced me, called me a murderer. Violent. Stubborn. But it's the reverse. He took my Kingdom. Plagued my people. Masked pain and suffering behind propaganda. Tortured me. Banished me to the depths of hell. Now, I shall return his actions tenfold. My allies. Undead. Dragons. Here to serve that meddling emperor a cold dish of what he deserves, and remove my people from his chessboard. I grabbed the horn. A deep breath, I blew. Unsheathing my sword, I climbed onto my horse, and my army started moving, a cacophony of vengeance.

Lance Lau
Brighton College, Brighton

GONE TURBO

I raced across the finish, closely followed by an elated cheer.
I leapt from my kart, waved and smiled at all my friends.
Hands patted me on the back whilst others reached for high-fives.
Gathering with everyone else I saw the game slowly merge into the socket. As it finally clunked into place three simple words flashed up in red: 'Speed Car Racing'.
I raced into the game overcome with jealousy. These high graphic nobodies really think they're better... I crashed thoughtlessly into a speeding car. We skidded around, red glitches surrounded us. What had I done?

Evie Stubbs (12)
Brighton College, Brighton

TIME FOR REDEMPTION

It was a dream come true, the Volksfrei had accepted me into their powerful movement. However, one small mistake and my dream got crushed.

I have been plotting my redemption for many years, but now is the time. Now everyone will know the name... Hans Gruber.

All of America was screaming in fear for the hostages held in Nakatomi Plaza. My petrifying redemption plan was going perfectly until that scoundrel they call John McClane swooped in to save the day.

My wealth, my name but most importantly my life all ended because of the New York cop, John McClane.

Theo Elyas (13)
Brighton College, Brighton

SECOND BEST

But of course, I'm not good enough to live up to my brother. The God of Thunder. Thor this, Thor that. I've had enough of being 'second best'.

They don't know what I've been through, what I have had to do to get even the tiniest of recognition. They will never know. To everyone else, I am the 'rich, spoiled, mischievous Prince of Asgard'. That's not true, That's not what I am. I am Loki, God of Mischief and I will not take this anymore.

Just because Odin favours Thor, doesn't mean I can't rise, I will get my revenge...

Iliana Savvidou (13)
Brighton College, Brighton

THE TRUTH BEHIND MY ACTIONS

You may think I'm mad, perhaps you believe I've no reason for my evil doings but that's untrue. Mother took me to get candyfloss one day at the fair; as I watched the lady stir it came to my attention, my mother had vanished.

Perhaps she left for the toilet, I thought to myself, so I sat on one of the benches and waited.

Years I waited; she wasn't returning... Why should I alone have to age without a parent? I shouldn't! That's why I have been separating children from their families, so they can suffer just as I did.

Katherine Green (12)
Brighton College, Brighton

THE BEGINNING OF DARTH VADER'S END

I entered the chamber and there he was. It was my son, Luke Skywalker. Next to him, sitting proudly on his throne, was Palpatine. Luke's plan was to destroy the Death Star, but he knew that Palpatine and I couldn't let that happen. Suddenly, Luke dived at me, lightsaber drawn out. Luke swung at me with such skill and precision. He had been trained well. I swiped at him but his defence was quick. The next thing I saw was the bright, fluorescent green of his lightsaber. My instinct was to block it, but I was unsuccessful. My hand was gone.

Caleb Lawrence (12)
Brighton College, Brighton

THE ENCOUNTER

On the morning of the encounter, I was tending to my sheep as usual. The youngest lambs were still demanding attention, bleating and calling me back into the field whenever I was about to leave. When I eventually managed to descend without interference, it was already nearing midday.

As I reached the last few steps, I saw something I never expected. In my own home, there was a band of what seemed to be sailors, tearing into my food supply like vultures. I knew that my hospitality was well-known, but how could I be expected to put up with this?

Oliver Geer (14)
Brighton College, Brighton

YOU THOUGHT I'D FORGET?

You thought I'd forget? Forget what you did?

I remember you forcing me into the woods after school, the insides of your satchel jingling on your hip, I could only imagine the contents: knives?

You pinned me down at twilight, my head hitting the roots hard; wincing in pain, I watched you draw something out of your bag, it glinted in the moonlight. You skimmed the cold steel blade against my throat before tying me to a tree.

I took my last breath.

Now my soul wanders the forest, searching the mists and moulds, waiting to haunt your earthly body.

Amalisse Mansoubi (13)

Brighton College, Brighton

RED-FACED

Another impact. This time in my right eye. A couple of hours later, they blind me by setting up a big inflatable tent, their HAB. They drive around for five days.

I lost it. I blew my top, literally. A huge sandstorm whips up and within half a day they're all gone. Except one. These humans are so stubborn!

128 years ago, humans first put a lander on my jawbone. I was enraged!

Nothing escapes me.

549 days later.

The only way I could get this man off of me was by helping him.

So, he's gone.

Peace at last.

Mo Xu
Brighton College, Brighton

THE BIG BAD WOLF: PRELUDE

The big bad wolf plodded up the hill, finally making it to the top, then taking out his inhaler when three little pigs came and violently snatched it off him!

He raced off after them but was too out of breath to run for long. He trudged on.

Finally, he reached the first two pigs' houses made of straw and sticks, which promptly fell down when he politely knocked on the weak door. Both the pigs fled to the last house, made of brick. From there they jeered and laughed at the poor wolf. Then, three more pigs came along.

Dylan Quinn (12)
Brighton College, Brighton

STELLA CADENTE

I killed someone. Does this make me a villain? Does this make me bad? No. People just don't understand me. My victim entered my territory. Stole my food. I am described by people as someone with killer instincts, who hurts anyone who challenges me. I was born that way. I kill for egoism. If I didn't, I would be the one who's six feet underground. I would be the one they would all be mourning. I should not be called names like 'murderer'. I hunt and I kill. My name is Stella Cadente. I am a cat, not a villain.

Astrid Facius (12)
Brighton College, Brighton

REMEMBER THE LIGHT

Why don't they understand me? I reach up the slope and pull myself up once more. Wailing in agony I lie there, still. Writhing in pain I wake on an icy table. The torment intensifies as droids start to repair my singed flesh. I scream in agony until prosthetic limbs are secured in place. I struggle to breathe as my burnt lungs start to give in. I'm lifted and placed into a cold, metal suit. A dark helmet, put over my head. I take my first, slow, artificial breath. I try to remember the light but he is too strong.

Jake Penrose (13)
Brighton College, Brighton

THEIR STEPMOTHER

We decided to leave them in the middle of the woods. However, somehow, they still managed to come back. Their father was happy, of course, (he was against us leaving them), I had to act as if I was too. I wasn't. They were a nuisance, always asking me to play with them, I mean, why would I be bothered to?

Anyway, a few days later I decided to do it again. Last time, Hansel brought along some rather shiny pebbles which he threw on the ground so he could see his way back home. This time, that's not happening...

Dhanya Reddivari
Brighton College, Brighton

DEAD SMELL

I blame my mother for the way I am. Sick, that's what she was. She would lock me in this dark cupboard and sever my fingers and toes. And again, straight after they had regenerated. And again, and again. Every single day.
I could never quite understand what drove her to do this. Maybe she was just a sadist, causing me pain for her own pleasure. Since the day I ran away, I have tried to control it. The urges I feel. Some days I see humans.
It's all her fault. The corpses in my basement have started to smell.

Sol Ghosh
Brighton College, Brighton

THE BETRAYED KINGDOM

People think I'm amazing, they are inspired by my 'kind heart' and angelic ways. Ever since that night I have felt the guilt of the world on my shoulders. I, heir to the throne of Merdia, killed someone.

I really did not mean any harm; I just could not handle the abuse any longer... they controlled and tracked every one of my thoughts. What if the secret got out that I was the perpetrator? It would be chaos. That is why I must flee to save the people from what I had done. I am doing it for my kingdom.

Orla Huzinga
Brighton College, Brighton

PAYBACK

I can never forget the time when the knight came to take my gold. They call me the fierce evil dragon, The greedy knight climbed up my lovely tower. He is back with many other people. Why can I not just live in peace, away from annoying 'knights' who rob dragons for fame? I have decided to put an end to this ridiculous man. I will lure him into my tower, and he will get greedy as he fills up his gold pouch. I will come from behind and teach him a lesson. I can hear him already. Ha, ha...

Peterson Ouyang
Brighton College, Brighton

THE MAGICIAN

I was an entertainer, who used powers, but I was treated poorly. One day, a fire broke out in the carnival. I saw the person who had set the fire, but the detectives could not find the cause so they blamed it on me. This person, the now-famous superhero, had stolen my powers.

Years later, I was finally on the verge of finishing my speed potion to do anything in my power to gain popularity. But he captured me in a capsule of dark matter and it corrupted my potion and the Earth fell dark.

Noel Yang
Brighton College, Brighton

THE CAKE

I still had to make up for what I'd done. Lyra could never forgive me, I just wanted her to be safe. I came back from a long day working and went up the lift to my flat, as the door slid open I mustered a smile as genuine as I could manage. We went to sit in the living room. I gave her a slice of the cake that I had carefully prepared earlier that day. She unwittingly took a bite, drowsiness came over her quickly as I'd hoped. I breathed a sigh of relief; my plan was working.

Miranda Ellicock
Brighton College, Brighton

MEET AMONG THE STARS

The world goes dark. Flames envelop me. It is not painless, as the warriors say.

I made sure his was painless. I made sure he died unknowing of my pain, my secret hate of him, of my father, of my name. But I know he never meant it. Mufasa was just scared. I understand. And yet, I am the one who became his beast. Perhaps I do deserve this.

So, as my hand slips, I hope I am caught by him. I close my eyes and with my dying breath, I pray to meet him in the stars.

Cassady Lovell (13)
Brighton College, Brighton

THE EXPERIMENT

He promised me greatness and lied. I had cancer. The doctor told me I had two hours to live. I walked out of the hospital and bumped into a guy named Dr Zy. He told me he could cure me and give me powers that nobody has ever had. I agreed. I followed him to his lab and he put me to sleep. When I woke up, I didn't see Dr Zy anywhere, I looked down and then I realised I was a monster. I found a cave in the middle of nowhere. There I slowly planned my revenge.

Yuwen Liu (12)
Brighton College, Brighton

INNOCENT

I wasn't trying to hurt anyone! This girl is dangerous, I was just trying to save the innocent civilians of this town! You see, this all started when this girl opened a portal to a very dangerous dimension. Eleven nearly killed us all! Very dangerous monsters came climbing out of this very portal! An exit for the dangers that lie beneath. That is the reason that I am keeping this girl in lockdown. Also, those horrible rumours about me kidnapping this child are wrong, this is my child. I am her Papa caring for her whilst she is isolating.

Maisie Berry (11)
Chipping Sodbury School, Chipping Sodbury

THE CHRISTMAS WISH

Everyone says I'm evil. I'm not. I hate Christmas. Everyone sings songs and gives presents. It's horrible! One day I went shopping and this pathetic girl sang in front of me. I said I hate singing. I had a devilish idea. I was going to steal Christmas!
I did as planned but I saw the same girl. She asked what I was doing and I said stealing Christmas. She said how lovely it was. I stopped and thought. Christmas wasn't that bad after all! I shouted, "I wish I loved Christmas," and it came true. I love it so much!

Ellie-Mai Stange
Chipping Sodbury School, Chipping Sodbury

THE EVIL REVENGE

I used to love Christmas. Everything about it. The lights, trees and parties until one day somebody spoiled it. Destructive people. On Christmas, no one cared about me. I was isolated. Depressed. And shut out. I wanted revenge! So I did. I took their magical Christmas away. Their favourite season. All I had to do was wait for the perfect time. When the clocks struck midnight, it was my time to steal their joy. I took their Christmas spirits. You see they shut me out. Made me follow my plan. So now I hate Christmas. Everything about it!

Erin Kirby (12)
Chipping Sodbury School, Chipping Sodbury

THE THING ABOUT DALMATIANS

Cruella was a standard child. She did what you asked without complaining but somehow this darling child became Satan. Cruella was so sweet and she knew what she wanted, she wanted a dog to play with; her mum got her a Dalmatian puppy. When she saw the dog she was very happy.

A few years later she entered her dog (Spotty) into a competition and she won almost every single category, but then all the Dalmatians (fifteen of them) turned and ran after her. Ever since that dreadful day she vowed that Dalmatians won't grow up...

Charlotte Davies (12)

Chipping Sodbury School, Chipping Sodbury

THE DEVILISH PLAN

People know me as the taunting person who stole Christmas but that's not who I am at all. A long time ago, people called me horrible names and made me leave my town onto a hill just outside. Alone. That's when I started to plot my evil revenge on these horrible people. First, I had to find something they took away from me. Christmas. When my devilish project was ready I had to wait until Christmas eve! When it was time I proceeded to the plan. So you see they pushed me to my demonic plan. These idiotic, selfish people.

Elaya Brown (11)
Chipping Sodbury School, Chipping Sodbury

LOKI LAUFEYSON

I never really belonged in my family. I was rather mischievous and though I, to some extent, was loved by them, they didn't pay much attention to me. After finding out the truth about myself, I began to realise how... pitiful my life was.

I took my anger out on my father and brother, well, until I faked my death for the first time. I came back a few years later and sided with villains, which led to fighting The Avengers. After being defeated by them, I went on siding with my brother, playing a few tricks along the way.

Mia Williams (14)
Chipping Sodbury School, Chipping Sodbury

JUST ONE BITE

Everyone says I'm evil, my story is different. I was in mid-life and found my lover. It was perfect, until my dreadful wedding eve. The enchantress came bursting through my door claiming my lover was hers. I was devastated but my lover denied it. The witch was raging. She cursed both of us. She trapped my lover in a mirror. And for me, I was given a heart of stone. I was emotionless. Driven crazy with grief, found myself a rich husband and had a daughter. She reminded me of myself; I hated her. I called her Snow White.

Molly Andrews (12)

Chipping Sodbury School, Chipping Sodbury

KING

"I was a king. Now I'm locked up. I tried to balance both worlds. But when menace meets, you can't get rid of them. I've got no one but I will get out. I'm being punished for a crime I didn't commit and when I do I'll have his head, this is the end game and it will be yours, you've met your match and we're ready. I will destroy you! You ruined my life and now I'll ruin yours. Think of all the lost lives you thought you were saving. Just you wait Spider-Man! See you soon Peter."

Declan Prosser
Chipping Sodbury School, Chipping Sodbury

THE GRINCH

"I never really belonged there, Max. All those perfect Whos and I'm just a green slob. Oh well. I'll make them feel how I felt that day. It was horrible Max. Everyone, including me, brought in gifts. I had made an angel out of metal and gems. It was for a girl but everyone laughed, it was horrible. So I threw the tree out the window and knocked the gifts over, they were cheap anyway. I never really had anyone to rely on. It's sad. Max, are you listening? I will make sure all those Whos pay the price."

Channon Dracup (14)
Chipping Sodbury School, Chipping Sodbury

PAINFUL PAST

I was loved twice, but that was a long time ago. My mother loved me and would tell me joyous stories. Every day I witnessed my wicked father abuse my mother and I watched in pure horror. One day, out of nowhere, she died and that devastated me. For a moment my world broke, and then Clair came into my life. She had fixed broken pieces. But that didn't last long. When my father found out, he killed her.

I was furious. I knew that my father was just envious, but that didn't matter. So, I planned my devilish plan...

Sophie Brady (11)
Chipping Sodbury School, Chipping Sodbury

BROKEN HEART

There's a reason why I'm evil. It all started when I was fifteen. There was a boy. His name was Charles. We were deeply in love. Every day he would sit outside and give me a white rose. But one day... he left. He found this disgusting half-human, half-animal creature and fell in love with her. Her name was Alice. From then on, I despised animals and cut off the heads of people in love. I covered my garden with every colour of rose apart from white. Any animals that entered my wonderland would become my slaves.

Amelie Gwynn (12)
Chipping Sodbury School, Chipping Sodbury

THE LAST LAUGH

When I was twelve, it all approached the stage I dreaded most. Secondary school. My father had told me the foreboding path ahead. But suddenly, the ship sunk. Every day, I would receive a shouting at, a beating. Although this would all change. It was time to change, for good.
No longer would I suffer, I would make them suffer! To begin with, all I did was rob some banks and kill some people and I ended up in an asylum. I was demonic! I couldn't be stopped! Until he came, Batman. Now I know who I am, a villain...

Jacob Shipp (11)
Chipping Sodbury School, Chipping Sodbury

TALE OF THE EVIL NORMAN OSBORN

I was born without an arm. I've been trying to find a way to grow it back. It's been twenty years since I started trying to grow it back and I still haven't found a way.

A boy came in and told me an equation that I needed, but the only person that I knew had the equation was Tom Parker. But he was dead. I realised who it was. Peter. Tom's son. I tested the equation on hundreds of things, but none of them worked. Suddenly, something worked!

The next day, I became a devilish monster lizard.

Riley Wakefield (11)
Chipping Sodbury School, Chipping Sodbury

THE STORY OF EDDIE BROCK

One day, I was taking a walk in the woods. I saw some weird black sludge on the floor. I touched it and then... "We are Venom!" I felt different, I felt devilish. Turns out the police were looking for it. When they were near, the satanic sludge made me jump into a tree. "Argh" They couldn't find me. My plan was to jump from tree to tree back to my apartment. When 'we' got back, *bish, bash, bosh* there were people in there. "I need to get this out of me..."

Jed Rundle (12)
Chipping Sodbury School, Chipping Sodbury

THE LAUGHING BAT

Once I was the hero of Gotham but now I am a horrific demon! It all started when the Joker finally made me snap... his neck, I regret that every day. The second Joker died, he released toxic and infectious gas, it was horrifying. When I first felt the effects I felt weird and then... I smiled. That was when I killed them... all of them, the Justice League, the entire rogues gallery even the Green Lantern Corps, they were dead, all of them, even the gods themselves fell against my guns. Then it all ended!

Eli Phelan (11)
Chipping Sodbury School, Chipping Sodbury

VENOM

I was a weak symbiote. Every single day I was bullied on a maroon planet. So they kicked me off and sent me out to space until I saw a beloved planet, Earth. It was very strange at first; there were tons of humans that I could devour.

One at a time they dropped, blood squelching out until there was one that I wanted to control! No one will notice. My vicious fangs smashed into bones, killing all kinds at a Chinese party. The more I eat, the more powerful I am. But now, I wanted revenge on the symbiotes.

Finley Griffee (11)
Chipping Sodbury School, Chipping Sodbury

AN APPLE

I had a hard life as a child. Bullied and abused. In school and at home. People were demonic. People would call me horrific, cruel and ugly.

One lunch, I bit my apple. It tasted funny. I began to feel dizzy, the world was spinning around me. Poison! The apple was poisoned. As I fell to the ground I saw Amanda staring at me laughing. She had short black hair tied with a red ribbon.

They left me to die. I didn't die. Of course. I was furious. But I have found her daughter. Now I plot my revenge!

Magda Wickiewicz (11)
Chipping Sodbury School, Chipping Sodbury

THANOS

I'm having a day off from depleting the population by a third. As I walked round my ship, getting saluted by my army, I realised how depressed my life is... Suddenly! We were getting attacked, by my old planet! I thought, *this is my time for revenge...*

I laughed viciously. I got my gear on and ran to the door to see that he was there. I opened the window and started spraying my laser rifle! So did my army. We picked them all off. At last, I have had my revenge.

Finlay Jouxson (14)

Chipping Sodbury School, Chipping Sodbury

DEMONIC HEART

Batman had finally thrashed the Joker, but then gas came out. Batman inhaled the gas and turned into a Batman who laughs.

One night he finally saw them, the Justice League, having a party that the Joker's dead. He swore to kill every last hero until he dies.

Then one night he did it. He had killed every person in the universe. He had won as the last one standing. As the fiend came to a stop another villain came!

His plan was about to commence...

Cole Rogerson (12)

Chipping Sodbury School, Chipping Sodbury

THE PATH NO ONE WANTS TO TAKE

"Am I...dead?"

"Indeed," the Grim Reaper answered, "we are walking to your afterlife."

"No! This can't be happening! I want to live!"

The woman, realising her situation, threw a fit. The Grim Reaper, who was leading the way all this time, suddenly stopped. "Doesn't eternal slumber sound satisfactory to a person who worked their whole life? You seek salvation in your lifetime, yet curse it when it's presented to you in a form you're unfamiliar with. Don't villainize Death, it isn't evil to you: it's just that no one told it that it, in fact, was, from your perspective."

Mariia Lysenko (15)
D'Overbroecks College, Oxford

SACRED

His expression faltered. Guilt, acquiescence, and a little loneliness appeared beyond the horizon. He would've welcomed a vindictive, violent disparagement. Questions... less so.

"The only ones I let continue are those still tangled in the strings. Chances are that you'd die there and there'd be one less god to deal with. I wish you all the best."

In a final stroke of desperation: "Please. We're sacred. Sacred!"

He let out a sigh.

"Heroes come to resemble the gods they fight for and nothing beyond that. Forsaken, left to rot, bumbling in the wild; undead, unfree. And nothing else besides."

Sze Long (15)
D'Overbroecks College, Oxford

SHE

Since I was born, I never really belonged to these ordinary people, I was unique. (My mum told me this.) So before Cruella, I used to be called Estella. Estella was a normal girl, who had a dream but couldn't make it come true because she was too introverted. Lots of people think I'm a dreadful person and Id don't deserve to live. But who are they? I'm an independent woman with great prospects. Fashion is my passion and nobody can be allowed to stand in my way. I'm Cruella de Vil... bold, brilliant, born bad and a little mad.

Alisa Arkharova (13)
D'Overbroecks College, Oxford

THE LONELY SNAKE

Medusa never really belonged, nobody wanted to go near her nor look at her. Those who gazed into her eyes would turn into stone. She was beautiful and it was that beauty of hers that cursed her forever. She was lonely and always wanted someone to talk to. However, whenever people met her, they would scream and run away. There were also people who weren't afraid and didn't run away but as soon as their eyes met, the curse started and the living snakes on her head turned them into stone, leaving Medusa alone again.

Jun Theppadungporn (14)
D'Overbroecks College, Oxford

THE STORY OF LOKI

I wasn't an Asgardian. I was adopted by Odin from the Iced Giants which made me an outcast. Nobody would talk to me and my brother, Thor, was a bully. There was one thing I wanted, the crown. I wanted to be king so people would accept me but with Thor and Odin, it was impossible. So I contacted the Ice Giants to attack and I negotiated a deal, so when they take Asgard I can be king. So the time has come and I open the Bifrost Bridge. There rush thousands of Ice Giants ready to take Asgard.

Derrick Lam (14)
D'Overbroecks College, Oxford

MY REDEMPTION

I had to make up for what I'd done. A hundred years ago, I attacked the village and I lost. I had to go back to my home and have a peaceful life. But Master Dogway and Po didn't want to leave me alone. They tried to attack my home. They killed my friends, my family. They destroyed my home. I tried to stop them but they were too strong and I had been defeated. They killed all life in my village. They destroyed everything. They caught me, took me to their prison and starved me to death.

Howard Pang (14)

D'Overbroecks College, Oxford

THE TRUTH BEHIND COVID

Hi, I'm Covid, I've had enough of what humans are doing. They are constantly killing billions and trillions of viruses. I thought humans were kind, how dare they kill us! Because of that, it has made us very mad, it's time for me to evolve into a stronger, better, bigger, more mighty virus! It's time for us to conquer the world! It's time for us and my fellow viruses to build a great dynasty and kill all the humans! I'm waiting for you, fools.

Harry Wang (13)
D'Overbroecks College, Oxford

THE HEIST

One frightful Thursday morning in New York City, Ellis'
phone rang unexpectedly. He answered it, and a voice said,
"I have a job for you. Worth 1.2 million dollars."
Without hesitation, Ellis replied, "I'm in!"
That night, Ellis was given the details of the job. The
National Bank was the location, a gigantic stone-faced
building with bright red curtains in all the windows.
Excitement, anxiety was high, however, the pull of money
outweighed the risk, and the job was on. Ellis strolled into
the bank, pulled down his mask, shot into the air and yelled,
"Get on the ground!"

Hayden Gell (14)

Danesgate Community PRU, Danesgate

ANGUISH OF THE BLIND

He was stranded with nothing but fragmented memories - the ghosts of a hollow heart's ruptured hope. Soothing stories battling eternal haze devolved into deranged voices declaring villainy. *Why'd he abandon them?* Disembodied cries of guilt fused with fog, contorting into fume-forged figures he fretted were forever forgotten. *"You've no blood or bone! You're figments of my sorrow!"* He fought the fog in a voracious frenzy, expelling the masquerading imposters. Hunkering down, back against a monolithic spire of rotting bark, he saw the haze clear... corpses bathed in the rancid stench of despair as sharp realisation struck him. *Were they real?*

Stefan Pinzaru (14)

Dixon Fazakerley Academy, Aintree

THE VILLAIN AND THE HERO

There was once a great battle where many people, good and bad, died. Only two people remained - Hero and Villain. They knew there was no point in fighting yet they continued. Hero wanted peace but Villain wanted revenge, both knew that this was impossible. Villain and Hero clashed day and night, hoping the fighting would end.

On a day just like any other day, a ferocious battle began. Suddenly, Hero fell and with his last breath said, "The fighting needs to stop. It is a fight no one can win. Please." Hero died in Villain's arms. Villain was left alone.

Wealth Okojie-Aiyagbonrhuele (14)

Dixon Fazakerley Academy, Aintree

STRINGS ATTACHED

I hopelessly dangle from my strings - the constant reminder of my imprisonment. My own puppeteer makes me kill innocent people for his enjoyment and I pray that people stay away.

I see the door creak open and another innocent soul wanders in. He glares at my hanging body and does nothing to help me. As the young man turns his back, I feel my strings pull, forcing me to grab a knife. But this time, I don't comply and with all my strength, I cut my own strings.

I crash helplessly to the floor. I saved myself. I'm free.

Louie Dunbabin (14)
Dixon Fazakerley Academy, Aintree

THE WOLF'S STORY

I wasn't always the monster you see me as today. I lived a peaceful life until one night...

I was cutting down a tree when something appeared ahead. It was a wolf that was as dark as the night sky. I froze in terror as it ran towards me. In one motion, I swung my axe and chopped off the beast's head. In the motion, I was bitten and old tales told me that I would too become a wolf by midnight. Soon, everything changed.

Now I live a lonely life, but I have one thing and that is hope.

Marty McCarthy (14)
Dixon Fazakerley Academy, Aintree

THE REALM OF DARKNESS

I never really belonged here, in this demonical realm of darkness. The deprived dense air convulsed through my jagged proportioned tongue. Horrid screams of my victims expulsed as I feared of complexed thoughts. "Why me?" I moaned in an undefined tone. My black lustrous cape sensed my cracking, appalling skin. I held a tenebrous rake filled with corpses eerie souls as the preternatural gestures of bloodthirsty gargoyles follow my path towards the 'never land'. "Help me! This was a mistake!" I cried. No one replied. There is no sense of hope in here. It's as silent as death.

Tsz Yin, Isaac Lee (13)
Eastbourne College, Eastbourne

THE INTERVIEW

My anger began to grow to the size of mountains, planets, galaxies. "I'm not a maniac," I cried. "Why does nobody believe me?" The interviewer stared at me, mocking my existence, twisting my words. "I didn't mean to kill her," my voice exploded.

"Then who did you mean to?" His voice tremored with anger.

"You," I screamed. Blood streamed out of my eyes, over my hands. I felt the urge to run, but it was checkmate. The only difference was that if I really were innocent, I would be either white or black. In this case, I'm covered in red.

Lucy O'Hara

Eastbourne College, Eastbourne

INVISIBLE THREAT

"Who's the real villain?" you might ask, well let me introduce myself to you. Viruses, infections and diseases make everyone distraught and discombobulated. I'm as invisible as can be, a threat to everyone that no one knows exists. As revenge travels across my mind, draconian or solemn there's always someone who dies because of this anger in me. Infected or not they're always afraid of me. All I see are human beings and animals in my surroundings. Emotions running through my head. Around me, the sounds of coughing and choking are some of the side-effects I inflict on people.

Serena Ting (14)
Eastbourne College, Eastbourne

CONFESSIONS OF A SERIAL KILLER

No one knows I'm dying. Nobody knows I'm being utterly consumed by this guilt. I have been suffering alone, my voice restrained from calling for help. It wasn't my fault, how could it be? There is someone else involved. The constant feeling of repulsive self-loathing overflows my inner self and infects my bitter heart; the one part of me that was still sane until it drowned in hatred and died. Dead, a devastating thought. Think, the last thing you do before you die. Love, a dangerous thing that kills. I'm sorry Father, please forgive me... or take me with you.

Poppy Campion (13)
Eastbourne College, Eastbourne

HERO?

The TV buzzed with the cruel words of the ostentatious reporter. "Another meaningless death at the hands of..." I launched the controller at the TV, sparks flew, for a moment it was beautiful, but it faded as most things do. "They do not understand! Do they think I enjoy it... I don't, do I? I... I do it for them! More people equals less food, less food equals eventual extinction. I should be called a hero, not..." I paused, "a villain."
I stood up, the soft cloud of dust crept out of the chair to follow me out the door.

Felix Boyes
Eastbourne College, Eastbourne

THE LAST BLAST

I stopped. Suddenly it hit me. I looked down regrettably. Blood. Shrieking. Death. I released the gun. The clatter was deafening. In front of me lay death. Soaked in the claret-red of blood. There was someone lying there in agony. Pain. Her eye was no more. I strode through the bloodbath. People running, screaming all around me. It was me. They were running from me. I wanted to run. I couldn't. I stopped. My family. They wouldn't be proud. I heard the sirens. I saw the gun. Picked it up. Pressed it against my head. Pulled the trigger.

Orlando Soucek (13)

Eastbourne College, Eastbourne

THE MURDER

Scampering up the stairs after hearing my sister scream in agony. My heart pounded out of my chest. I charged to her room, grasped the handle of the door, twisted it and then a glacially freezing shiver made its way up my spine. The knife pierced through her paper-white skin, the scarlet blood seeped down her face, oozed onto the stone floor. There was a trail of blood meandering out of the door. I seized the knife from her body. The walls were suffocating, slowing me down. The lights flickered. Spying the murderer, I drew the knife back...

Olivia Wilson (14)
Eastbourne College, Eastbourne

BONES

Dark, skeletal branches surrounded me, like an aura of death, but I loved it, they reminded me of myself. The caw of crows was like a symphony to me, I know, how stereotypical. You know, you would think that I'd get a bit bored of draining the life out of people after doing it for millions of years but there's just something so emancipating about it all, all those twisted and tangled memories, all the weird and wonderful things that that person had seen and done just flow like a piece of paper-thin silk into my rotting bones.

Emilia Dixon (13)
Eastbourne College, Eastbourne

DON'T RELEASE ME

In the tube, there was something wrong. When I was let off the leash I knew I would cause damage, bumping along the surface with my antennae sticking like tentacles. My brothers, swarming around unsuspecting prey, they try and blow us out but the damage has been done. We then move to the next like a shark. We are like the needle in a haystack. People panic, people die, we have no feelings but we didn't want harm but they released us and we got hungry for blood like a shark with his devilish bat, sucking people's lives away.

Myles Luther (13)
Eastbourne College, Eastbourne

TIME

Clocks ticking. Hands turning. Why do I get the blame?
Watching the strong become weak. Watching the young
become withered. What is the point? To be born, to grow up,
to impact civilisation. And then to die. I watch humanity
evolve. I see the highs and the lows. But things have to
change to carry on living. Fresh ideas need to be introduced.
If no one died, humanity wouldn't evolve. Then what is the
point? To live forever. There is a point when death is a wish.
You need time to maintain the order of the world. You need
time.

Theo Hazlewood (14)
Eastbourne College, Eastbourne

THE VILLAIN?

Who really is the villain? Why am I thought of as a villain? My name is unknown to the public, to most people I'm an ordinary person living an ordinary life. Killing is just a hobby of mine, everyone has their hobbies, don't they? It gives an enormous rush of excitement like a huge wave of adrenaline crashing into me. A quiet life is all I ask for, no stress of people around me. I never wanted to, but I had no choice, the demon around my neck whispers words, "Kill, kill, kill, kill." I just wanted to be happy.

Dom Muschialli (13)
Eastbourne College, Eastbourne

THE WITNESS

My thoughts went back to that moment. I can still feel that cold sensation now of the freezing snow and air. That morning, that minute, those gunshots impregnated into my thoughts. I saw images in my head and looked at the witness. His face scarred, his clothes, old and haunted. My eyes followed the smooth oiled wood towards Judge Romesh, staring at me grimly. My anger was silent. I knew I was in the wrong but there was something to win. We both had told our stories. It was just like on the battlefield but this time in court.

Nicholas Beech
Eastbourne College, Eastbourne

THE KILLER'S ESCAPE

Heart racing, adrenaline pulsing through my veins, I had just killed a man. I needed to escape from my life. I was as good as dead anyway, It was always just me in my cold, damp and dilapidated flat. I packed a bag with my savings from behind the loose corroding red brick in the wall. A cold breeze whipped my face like leather as I stepped off the bus. Head down, I walked into the woods. Tall, towering, twisted trees surrounded me; their bone-like fingers entwined with one another. I ran as far from humanity as possible.

Nancy Revill
Eastbourne College, Eastbourne

HATE

I am the one true power. I am the one who rules the world, a shadow behind the main light. I snatch away the corrupting feeling of love and replace it with myself, a much more overpowering emotion that demands attention at all times. I do you a favour, make you strong and push away feelings of melancholy and regret. A facade, a face to hide you, make you feel strong. The one true emotion that never fades, and leaves its entrails everywhere. A reliable thought to lean on, to rely on. One emotion to rule them all.

Dan Clark
Eastbourne College, Eastbourne

VILLAIN OR HERO?

How am I the villain? Why are they the heroes? How are we any different? This isn't just my fault, I was simply doing it to survive. Is it really a crime to eke out a life on this brutal, apocalyptic desert we call our home. A few short years ago, our Earth was teeming with life, but these so-called heroes took the fight too far! I must now fight for my survival by fighting them too. Am I really the villain for trying to pick up the pieces after their horrific and painful mistakes. Am I really the villain?

Libby Thorley (13)
Eastbourne College, Eastbourne

MY FIRST AND LAST LOVE

For me, I feel ecstasy, that she was both my first and last love. With him, I empathise that he doesn't get the same ending, that he's enduring life without his colour palette. Yet I did what I needed to do, she was an artist, always glued to her canvas. I wanted to prove I understood how important it was to her now that she didn't want me; for blue I drowned her, for red I slid blades under her skin until she bathed in her blood, for purple, I beat her until her flesh blossomed like bellflowers.

Lily Michaelides (14)

Eastbourne College, Eastbourne

WHY ME?

I live alone in this world, isolated from interaction. I can't escape from the cycle of life although mine is continuously being renewed. Day by day insanity growing, now distant from normality. My job is a deed to be done, although the gruesome reality. There are no cheats to the game I play. I work nonstop and do what is needed but my name is always used in vain. I am always the demon to society, the antagonist to every man's life. Forced into blame, hiding in the shadows, no identity. Why me?

Bertie Kane (14)
Eastbourne College, Eastbourne

PERFECTIONIST

Ten, ten, ten, this man has ten obvious flaws, he's interrupting my quiet life to flaunt his unbearably obvious flaws, he needs to go, he needs to be removed, forcefully. This man he's, he's imperfect, he's flawed I can't even remember what he was saying anymore, it's been drowned out... no, in fact, I've been pulled under the water, suffocating but unable to get to the surface, forever drowning and suffocating at the hands of his flaws. Who's really the villain here?

Alex Pilsbury (14)
Eastbourne College, Eastbourne

NO ONE LISTENS

I ran past the bright city lamps like a flash, nowhere to hide, knowing there was no looking back from this, I needed to forget and move on, but it wasn't my fault, they made me do it, but many will disagree. I knew they would find me, I didn't want them to take me away, I didn't need their help. No one ever listened to me about anything, they all said I was crazy and I needed to leave, even my family believed this, so that's why I had to do what I did, I.. killed them... Every one.

William Bligh

Eastbourne College, Eastbourne

THE CURSE

"Argh!" I was taken from the street. I didn't know what was going on. A mysterious face-covered man called Ruskin said I was cursed. He said I needed to kill a certain person to break the curse. They released me and left me with a sniper with a silencer. I saw the person, I shot my shot. *Bang!* I shot him dead between the eyes. His briefcase fell to the floor and it was full of money. I felt dizzy and fell to the floor. I was back on the street they found me on.

Alfie Lulham (14)
Eastbourne College, Eastbourne

GUILT

The shrill sound of the gunshot pierced my ears. The hairs on the back of my neck stood up. A bitter shiver ran through my body. The body dropped. There is blood on my hands. He is dead now. My family are safe. So am I. People think badly of me for what I did. I did what I had to. They put the people I love in danger. Why me? Now I live with the guilt of taking an innocent life. I can never erase that image. The thought will loom in my head until the day I die.

Freddie Russell
Eastbourne College, Eastbourne

SLEEPING BEAST

Oh, here we are again. Maleficent. A villain who killed Aurora. Here's an update - Aurora didn't die. As I'm just sitting in this cell, I suppose I could tell you what actually happened.

I looked after that useless Aurora. Such a spoilt child, always complaining. Particularly about how the clothes I made her always fell apart. One day, I shoved that infuriating girl in front of the spinning wheel, to teach her how to do something for herself. That's what happened to me. Yes, she pricked her finger. Now she knows how I felt... except no prince saved me.

Grace Hill (14)

Felpham Community College, Felpham

NEVER TRUST A GENIE

It was uncomfortably hot the day the sultan sold his daughter to keep a secret. You would be wrong to assume Jasmine married for love. Her love rots in jail accused falsely of her mother's murder while the sultan knows the truth. The day Jafar supposedly killed her, a money-hungry street-rat watched but Aladdin didn't see Jafar. Instead, he saw the sultan looming over her body. To keep his secret, the sultan married off his daughter to Aladdin. She sorts out a genie to solve her problem but genies twist words. Jasmine now lies dead, her lungs full of sand.

Annalise Towse (14)
Felpham Community College, Felpham

HOW DID THAT HAPPEN?

I wouldn't have expected me to get caught! I thought I was in a secret lair, not an enormous pyramid in the middle of nowhere (which I think it was).

Gene Boy busted the door down and said that he had found me; or so he thought... Behind him marched his idiot sidekick, Duke Superb. "Urgh!"

They started walking down my very long hallway, not knowing what was going to happen next. Little did their stupid brains know that I had a button behind me that would drop my 'inescapable cage' onto them.

They didn't know it was coming...

Reece Bevan (12)
Felpham Community College, Felpham

TWISTED FAIRYTALE

Spun her straw to gold, 'twas returned with mere silver. As she forgets so blissfully it haunts me still. She wanders through life, loved without condition; but nowhere love is true, she is expecting... my child.

I have never been loved for how could the adored ever adore me? An imp, an outcast. They fear me always. But as my beautiful child opens its eyes for the first time, everything changes.

You never cared for my name but this child's name will be known throughout the land. I am Rumpelstiltskin, I am kind, I am strong, I am loved.

Katy Pilling (13)
Felpham Community College, Felpham

THE FALL

It was a normal morning for Jack. He got ready for the day and ate his cereal. When he finished his delicious Cheerios, he decided he wanted to go outside. Slowly he walked through the wet mud until he got to the Bean Walk higher than a skyscraper.

Jack looked it up and down and decided he would climb to the top. He started climbing and noticed it was a little bit slippy, but didn't take notice. As he got halfway it was getting very treacherous now. Suddenly he fell at the speed of light... *Thud.*

Max Broad (13)
Felpham Community College, Felpham

SYNDROME

Syndrome. He was who he was because of Mr Incredible. Just because he thought Syndrome was a normal boy. His name was Buddy Pine. All he desperately wanted to be was 'Incrediboy'. It was his biggest dream to be him. He came to me for a suit. I don't normally use capes but I did as he seemed very uneasy. Then he took on Mr Incredible. Violently, Jack threw him in the air. It was his last sight of everything. The cape I put on his suit got stuck in a plane engine. I was right to put it on.

Jacob Miles (13)
Felpham Community College, Felpham

THE FATHER'S SIDE OF THE STORY

Dear Diary,
This is Darth Vader. If you are reading this I am dead. It all started March 31st 2063. I was sleepwalking until I heard the door shut. It was Luke and his mother (my family). I don't know why people call me evil, I'm only trying to find my son.
Thousands of soldiers just like me have risked their lives just to help me in this quest. Sadly, when we did find him he just wanted to kill me. I didn't get the chance to tell him I missed him. My own son tried to kill me... Why?

Dylan Woods (13)
Felpham Community College, Felpham

MY LIFE

Yes, I was Mother Gothel. All the stories about my past well here's the truth... All I ever wanted to be was young and beautiful and to have a child of my own. But I never could have that as my time had passed.
Rapunzel was my only hope with a flower that I had loved and cared for, that Mother drank when she was giving birth. Her hair was long and silky and I dreamt of running my hands through it forever. That was going to keep me and how I always dreamed.

Scarlett Whittle (13)
Felpham Community College, Felpham

LITTLE MISS HUFF 'N' PUFF IT

I'm Mr J Spider. Spidy for short. I want you to understand it's all a mistake. Everything. Mostly...
'Little Miss Muffet,
Sat on her tuffet,
Eating her curds and whey'.
She certainly did; I'm not denying that.
'Along came a spider (that's me)
Who sat down beside her
And frightened Miss Muffet away!'
That's extremely harsh. There are countless mistakes with these lines. The claim that I joined her is unimaginably disgraceful. I was sitting there peacefully when she walked up, screamed, then ran away!
I reckon it's her fault, yelling like that. It's rude. The end. The proper end!

Verity Lowndes (13)
George Abbot School, Burpham

POWDER PLOT

My plan was in motion. Step one: gather the men to the start point near the cathedral. Get all gunpowder set in the underground barrels. Next, put the torches on fire and go underground. Finally, *bang,* our deed is done...

"Sir! There's a huge problem..."

"What?"

"The guards have found out..."

I drop the walkie-talkie, my hands shaking. "Commander... You still there?" I had nothing to say. I began to feel dizzy. The world spun around me and the next thing I know I had collapsed.

Our plan had failed. I let my team down; now we'll suffer the consequences.

Jasmine Lee (12)
George Abbot School, Burpham

DEAR DIARY (THE TOUCHING STORY OF A DEADLY THING)

Dear Diary,

Why? No one likes me. So what if I killed a few million people! Well, okay, I might have killed 5,262,849 but who's counting? Death made me to help and just set numbers straight, but stop blaming me! I am retired now. My remains are pumping them up!

Dear Diary,

Today was horrible. There was this foul human whom I hold grudge against. They stabbed me with a needle and I thought I found my safe haven. Mr Yeetus was a welcoming home until he stabbed me with a needle, I gasped for breath and was yeeted head-on...

Hayley Genge (11)

George Abbot School, Burpham

LONELINESS

As I sat and gazed at the misty moonlight over the mountains, I wondered. I wondered why the world was such a contradiction. I became infamous over a couple of nights. But I couldn't seem to understand why. Humans who were huge and strong were deathly scared of me, although I am invisible and powerless. My green, thorny appearance was only present to me. I wasn't really a villainous disease trying to destroy the world; I just had no choice. I have made my shelter perched atop a snowy mountain trying not to spread what I didn't have control of.

Manaswini Venugopal (12)

George Abbot School, Burpham

A WITCH'S DAY OFF

I'm having a day off from killing innocent people; it gets boring after a while. Someone knocked at the door. I answered it. He ran. I have to plan something a bit more extraordinary on my day off.

Sitting down on the sofa, I wrote down my rather interesting ideas until I came up with a best of the best idea. I can't hold it much longer, I will have to save my day off for another day.

Playing songs on my guitar on the streets, people stood around me until I shot everybody dead. Grinning to myself, I laughed.

Amber Grundy (11)
George Abbot School, Burpham

HELP!

Dear Diary,

They're not who you think they are. This is outrageous. Nobody ever listens to me. They are killing us faster than we can imagine! My family, my friends and more. We kill them only because they get too close, not for revenge! I can't just watch and do nothing but there is not much I can do. If this carries on, we will be 'wiped from the face of the earth in a few days'. This has to stop now! They chop our horns and use them for medicine. Without our horns we are vulnerable and we'll die.

Daniel Chen (11)
George Abbot School, Burpham

MISINTERPRETATION

The lavas of Mustafar gleamed in the twilight as he waited for his opponent to strike. Nothing. Through the devastation and chaos of the ruins, he saw the silhouette of his next victim. This was the person that had brought his former master here. To kill him. Or worse.

Hatred ran through his veins. He would enjoy this. He would enjoy this very much. He stabbed the figure before he could even think about it. It gasped, shocked and heartbroken. Its last expression of terror was still etched upon its face. Anakin looked into its empty eyes. Padmé looked back.

Joshi Lappin (13)
Haberdashers' Aske's Boys' School, Elstree

RE-VISIT

I never really belonged, never was good enough to be one of them, one of those... humans, even the word gives me shivers. That's why I broke away from them. The organisation took me, with great delight, I trusted them from the very get-go, they accepted me. It was a new thing for me, my first assignments were just normal. But then they turned me into something even I myself feared, looking into the mirror before each Christmas: those kids' faces before I take them for a 're-education', but they keep me on it. They always will. Forever. Krampus.

David Gluhovsky (12)
Haberdashers' Aske's Boys' School, Elstree

MAZEN MINOTAUR

"Where is he?"

"The Maze!" she cried!

I ran in, my head was high in the clouds, adrenaline carried me forward, turning corners, wildly throwing my body down the corridor, not even noting down my route.

There he was! The Minotaur! The towering beast stood over me like a skyscraper, his foul breath had a stench like gone-off milk. But I knew his secret. I knew why he ate people. He was depressed, he had no other source of food and he had not left the maze for twenty years. He had no friends, no family, and therefore no life.

Oliver Broadwith (13)

Haberdashers' Aske's Boys' School, Elstree

PETER PARKER THINKS AGAIN

Why should I protect the citizens? Why are all the police hiding? I'm the one with the power! I'm the best! I'm the one who feels the pain! This city is free of crime. At least, the meta-human type. I am the one and only meta and I will claim what is mine. I will command this universe and every other universe out there. Tonight, I shall seek my revenge. I shall take what they've all taken from me. I shall rise...

"We meet again, Red Skull. You stole all hope from me. You killed my parents! Prepare to die!"

Ishaan Shah (12)

Haberdashers' Aske's Boys' School, Elstree

THE VILLAINOUS HERO

Walking along the stage, waving my hand, basking in the applause for my heroic acts. However, deep down I knew I killed him, stopping a humble man from pursuing his dream, who wanted to help his beloved country; but there I stood over his corpse, witnessing the vermillion monster escape from his soul. Letting a hot tear drop down the side of my face onto the stone-cold body, I limply dropped down onto my knees, shaking him from side to side, trying to bring him back to life. There was nothing that could be done. I had killed my father.

Arav Bahel (13)

Haberdashers' Aske's Boys' School, Elstree

THE VICTIM WHO KILLED THE ASSASSIN

You heard me right. I'm a killer. Give me a knife or a pistol. I'll pull the trigger, but nobody asks why. You just lock me in a room with someone else and hope that I redeem myself. No! You ask me to pay for someone in a $5000 suit so he can argue with a person in a wig. Prove that I'm innocent. Ask people to take an oath to say only the 'truth'. Well, if you believe in the 'truth'.

When I attempt to escape, you extend my torture.

Why can't you just give me my beloved daughter?

Vivaan Chhabra (12)
Haberdashers' Aske's Boys' School, Elstree

ROBIN HOOD

It was the only way I could get away with it. By stealing from the rich and giving to the poor. But all I wanted was to steal some money and bathe in gold. The sheriff was a good friend of mine, the best of friends. But obviously, I had other plans. I had been wearing two masks at the same time, I just wanted to wear one, the mysterious man who stole from the Sheriff of Nottingham and become notorious and wealthy. Why should I lead a rebellion against the sheriff? It must have been someone else.

Louis Chew (13)
Haberdashers' Aske's Boys' School, Elstree

THE SERPENT IN A LION'S SKIN

For fifteen years, he was the valiant hero, while I was the notorious villain. I did what he wanted me to do. I wore what he wanted me to wear. I said what he told me to say. For I was the puppet and he was my puppeteer. But not once had he listened to me. He never asked what I wanted. But that would all change today. Today I would take back power from the snake that called himself the lion. I would expose him for the villain he truly was. But first I needed to escape this dungeon.

Harnek Tolani (12)
Haberdashers' Aske's Boys' School, Elstree

YoungWriters®
— Est. 1991 —

YOUNG WRITERS
INFORMATION

We hope you have enjoyed reading this book – and that you will continue to in the coming years.

If you're a young writer who enjoys reading and creative writing, or the parent of an enthusiastic poet or story writer, do visit our website **www.youngwriters.co.uk**. Here you will find free competitions, workshops and games, as well as recommended reads, a poetry glossary and our blog. There's lots to keep budding writers motivated to write!

If you would like to order further copies of this book, or any of our other titles, then please give us a call or order via your online account.

Young Writers
Remus House
Coltsfoot Drive
Peterborough
PE2 9BF
(01733) 890066
info@youngwriters.co.uk

Join in the conversation!
Tips, news, giveaways and much more!

 YoungWritersUK  YoungWritersCW 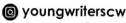 youngwriterscw